I Want To Be

Written and Illustrated by
Elizabeth Uhlig

MARBLE HOUSE EDITIONS

Published by Marble House Editions
96-09 66th Avenue (Suite 1D)
Rego Park, NY 11374

Library of Congress Cataloguing-in-Publication Data
Uhlig, Elizabeth
I Want to Be/by Elizabeth Uhlig

Summary: A rhyming book for young children about the pleasures of the
imagination.

ISBN 978-0-9815345-1-0
Library of Congress Catalog Card Number 2008902719

Printed in China

*This book is dedicated to the
memory of my mother,
Mary Freeman,
who loved creativity and fantasy,
and always embraced life.*

Each day when I get out of bed

I think about the day ahead.

What kind of magic will I see?

What will I do? Who will I be?

I let my 'magination play,
What am I going to do today....?

I'll go and ride my pet giraffe!

Or be a clown and make you laugh.

Some ice-cold lemonade I'll sell,

and you could ride the carousel.

Let's wear some fancy clothes and play, pretending it's our wedding day.

I'd like to see each far-off place, and wave to you from outer space.

I'll paint nice pictures just for you.

I'll see the monkeys in the zoo.

I want to dance, to be a tapper,

Me – I want to be a flapper!

I want to march in the parade,
and wear a suit with shiny braid.

I'll go and put a fire out,

I'll win a race – the crowds will shout!

I only want to watch my kite,
a-sailing like a bird in flight.

I'll see the fishes as I scuba,

Me – I want to play the tuba!

I might just take a walk and see the new
books at the library.

I'd like to ride a railroad train,

or just go splashing in the rain.

A ballerina I could be,
a-swirling, twirling gracefully.

But more
than these,
I want to spend
each day...

...with you,

and be
your friend.